All Scripture quotations, unless otherwise indicated, are taken from the following sources:

The Holy Bible, New International Version®, NIV®. Copyright ©1973,1978, 1984, 2011 by Biblica, Inc.™ Used by permission of Zondervan. All rights reserved. worldwide. www.zondervan.com The "NIV" and "New International Version" are trademarks registered in the United States Patent and Trademark Office by Biblica, Inc.™

Scripture quotations marked (AMP) are taken from the Amplified Bible, Copyright © 1954, 1958, 1962, 1964, 1965, 1987 by The Lockman Foundation. Used by permission.

Scripture quotations marked (NLT) are taken from the Holy Bible, New Living Translation, copyright ©1996, 2004, 2015 by Tyndale House Foundation. Used by permission of Tyndale House Publishers, Inc., Carol Stream, Illinois 60188. All rights reserved.

Scripture quotations marked (TLB) are taken from The Living Bible copyright © 1971. Used by permission of Tyndale House Publishers, Inc., Carol Stream, Illinois 60188. All rights reserved.

Scripture quotations marked MSG are taken from THE MESSAGE, copyright © 1993, 2002, 2018 by Eugene H. Peterson. Used by permission of NavPress. All rights reserved. Represented by Tyndale House Publishers, Inc.

Scripture quotations taken from the New American Standard Bible® (NASB), Copyright © 1960, 1962, 1963, 1968, 1971, 1972, 1973, 1975, 1977, 1995 by The Lockman Foundation. Used by permission. www.lockman.org. Scripture quotations marked TPT are from The Passion Translation®. Copyright © 2017, 2018 by Passion & Fire Ministries, Inc. Used by permission. All rights reserved. ThePassionTranslation.com. Scripture taken from the New Century Version®. Copyright © 2005 by Thomas Nelson. Used by permission. All rights reserved.

Scripture quotations marked EASY are taken from the EasyEnglish Bible Copyright © MissionAssist 2019 - Charitable Incorporated Organization 1162807. Used by permission. All rights reserved.

To

From

Date

Contents

Welcome 1

Introduction 2

Tips 4

Healing For Physical Pain 6

Healing For Invisible Wounds 8

Wisdom For The Medical Team 10

Faith To Embrace A Forgiving Heart 12

Protection From The Perpetrator 14

Deliverance From & Against Nightmares 16

Financial Provision For Medical Costs 18

Guidance During The Legal Process 20

Supportive And Reliable Resources 22

Backing From Another Survivor 24

Protection Against Re-Traumatization 26

Open Heart To Connect To God 28

Wisdom In My Decision Making 30

Open Eyes To See God's Direction 32

Strength To Love Again 34

Success In My Healing Journey 36

Reprieve From Negative Triggers 38

v

Willingness To Embrace God's Will 40

Patience With My Supporters 42

Hedge Of Protection Over My Children 44

PRAYERS FROM THE THREAD BOOK 47

Ability To Think Good Thoughts 48

Willingness To Learn From The Past 50

Help To Release The Trauma 52

Direction To Choose The Right Allies 54

Readiness To Adopt New Mindset And Behaviors 56

Desire To Dream Again 58

Commitment To Discover My Gifts 60

Desire To Live A Joyful Life In Christ 62

Courage To Walk In My Purpose 64

Freedom To Live True Happiness 66

Ephesians 1:18-20 TPT 68

Looking For More Resources 70

About The Author 71

Welcome

Release It offers 30 prayers for trauma survivors and supporters who are looking for a safe rest stop to converse with God in an honest, vulnerable, and transparent way. You are not alone! Find hope with these prayers as you rise above the trauma to start your journey to reclaiming your life. God's healing love is always available to you.

Maybe you already have an active prayer life, or you don't have one. Whatever the case, I welcome you to consider these prayers as a starting point to support your prayer life.

Never stop praying.
1 THESSALONIANS 5:17

INTRODUCTION

Part of healing from trauma involves acknowledging what you have been through and being real with yourself and God. As a trauma survivor of severe childhood abuses (sexual, physical, emotional, and spiritual), I know firsthand how damaging the aftermath of traumatic injuries are to the whole person (spirit, soul, mind, and identity).

In **Release It**, I share 30 prayers and journal prompts to help you engage in a personal conversation with God so He can heal the deep wounds of fear, shame, grief, and anger caused by trauma. If you've experienced severe trauma and are left feeling angry at God because He didn't intervene to stop or prevent the abuse, then you are not alone. I, too, have been there!

I wrote this prayer book to offer you a safe place to converse with God in an honest, vulnerable, and transparent way. *Release It* includes 30 prayers to help you and your supporters find hope and healing. Women's ministry groups can also use this book as part of their short-term bible study, retreat study, or as an introduction or follow-up to *The Thread: Let God into Your Heart and Achieve Intentional Transformation* book.

As you pray the scripture, you will discover five key things:

1. You are not alone! God loves you, and He wants to bring you healing from trauma.
2. You have access to the Father's promises, protection, and provision directly from His Word.
3. You can use prayer as a weapon to overcome obstacles that hinder your relationship with Jesus.

4. You will learn how to pray, let go of the pain in your past, and welcome a joy-filled life in Christ.
5. You do not need anyone's permission to enter and enjoy the life-changing presence of the Lord, and prayer is a refreshing way to get you there.

Women's ministry groups can also use this book as part of their short-term bible study, retreat study, or as an introduction or follow-up to THE THREAD: Let God into Your Heart and Achieve Intentional Transformation.

Get ready to release the pain in your past, as you transform from trauma and find healing and true freedom in Christ.

You are not alone. Find hope in these prayers as you rise and live your faith above trauma and start your journey to reclaiming your life. God's healing love is available to you today.

May everyone who knows your mercy keep putting their trust in you, for they can count on you for help no matter what. O Lord, you will never, no, never, neglect those who come to you.

PSALMS 9:10 TPT

TIPS

Here are a few things that will help you develop a routine or improve the one you already use:

1. Decide what results you want from your prayer time (for example, to hear from God about a specific issue you're facing) and write it down.
2. Prepare and plan a set time to meet with the Lord. Adjust distractions such as social media, TV, etc. If necessary, set the alarm on your device so you'll be reminded.
3. Keep your time doable, and make sure it works for you.
4. Read the bible Scripture and be sure to pray each daily prayer out loud.
5. Seek the Holy Spirit daily for empowerment and guidance, and as you do, ask the Lord, How am I to pray today?
6. Move more-depth into the presence of the Lord as you listen to understand what He has to say to you.
7. Use a personal journal to write down things you've heard from the Lord and need to surrender to God.
8. Remember, this is your time to learn from the Lord.
9. Be consistent in seeking and delighting yourself in Him and wait on Him to give you your heart's desires (Psalm 37:4).
10. Follow these simple daily instructions as you spend time pressing into God through prayer.

I believe that prayer is the key to unlocking our understanding of the power, purpose, and promises of God. My prayer is that you feel inspired to release everything that hinders you from receiving complete healing from trauma pain, fear, and memories, in Jesus's name. Enjoy your conversation with God, and do it as often as possible.

> *The confidence of my calling enables me to overcome every difficulty without shame, for I have an intimate revelation of this God. And my faith in him convinces me that he is more than able to keep all that I've placed in his hands safe and secure until the fullness of his appearing. Allow the healing words you've heard from me to live in you and make them a model for life as your faith and love for the Anointed One grows even more.*
> 2 TIMOTHY 1:12

May the Lord richly bless you!

Healing For Physical Pain

Wherever he went, in the countryside, villages, or towns, they placed the sick on mats in the streets or public places and begged him, saying, "Just let us touch the tassel of your prayer shawl!" And all who touched him were instantly healed!

MARK 6:56 TPT

God of Healing, I turn to You as I suffer from
physical wounds, pain, and heartache.
I turn to You because Your healing power is seen manifested in the scriptures: *The sick were laid in the marketplaces and begged that Your Son would let them touch even the fringe of His cloak. And all who touched Jesus were healed.* Lord, I am sick. I approach You with a faithful heart and ask for Your healing grace. Father, I thank You for healing me from physical wounds, pain, and heartache.

AMEN

Your Turn

My Gratitude List
Recount God's blessings today

Date: _____

Morning | Afternoon | Evening

My Prayer List
Surrender your concerns to God

Date: _____

Morning | Afternoon | Evening

Healing For Invisible Wounds

O LORD, if you heal me, I will be truly healed; if you save me, I will be genuinely saved. My praises are for you alone!
JEREMIAH 17:14 NLT

Heavenly Father, I pray for spiritual healing in my life right now as I struggle to cope because of my invisible wounds. I know that through You, I can be healed. Save me, and I shall be saved, for You are my praise. Lord, I ask that you treat me from the spiritual, emotional, and mental bondage that I am currently in. I declare healing over my life in Jesus' Name. Father, I thank You in advance for healing me from my invisible wounds.
AMEN

My Gratitude List Date: _____
Recount God's blessings today

Morning | Afternoon | Evening

My Prayer List Date: _____
Surrender your concerns to God

Morning | Afternoon | Evening

Wisdom For The Medical Team

*It is better--much better--to have wisdom
and knowledge than gold and silver.*
PROVERBS 16:16 GNT

Righteous God, I pray for the doctors and nurses that I meet on my journey of healing and medical advice. I pray that You fill them with wisdom rather than knowledge, as wisdom is the correct application of knowledge. Let them be sensitive towards my situation by approaching me with divine wisdom. Your word stresses how much better it is to get wisdom than gold, to get insight rather than silver. So, Father, please fill them with Your knowledge. Thank you, Jesus, for the wisdom of my doctor, nurses, and all medical specialists I encounter.

AMEN

Your Turn

My Gratitude List

Recount God's blessings today

Date: _____

Morning | Afternoon | Evening

My Prayer List

Surrender your concerns to God

Date: _____

Morning | Afternoon | Evening

Faith To Embrace A Forgiving Heart

*Then Jesus said, "Father, forgive them,
for they do not know what they do." And they
divided His garments and cast lots.*

LUKE 23:34 NKJV

Eternal God, I pray that You help me to embrace a forgiving heart. Honestly, this is a struggle for me because I have suffered so much from my trauma. It is hard to find genuine love and peace towards the one who harmed me, but I pray that You give me the strength to forgive my abuser. I pray that You increase my faith to do so. Let me be like Jesus, who, while being persecuted, cried out, "Father, forgive them, for they know not what they do." Help me embrace a genuinely forgiving heart. Thank you, Lord, for the faith to embrace a forgiving heart.

AMEN

Your Turn

My Gratitude List
Recount God's blessings today

Date: _____

| Morning | Afternoon | Evening |

My Prayer List
Surrender your concerns to God

Date: _____

| Morning | Afternoon | Evening |

Protection From The Perpetrator

*But the Lord is faithful; he will strengthen
you and guard you from the evil one*
2 THESSALONIANS 3:3 NLT

Almighty God, Your word says that anyone who hates is in the darkness and walks around in the dark. They do not know where they are going, because the darkness has blinded them. The perpetrator who hurt me and has kept media and information about me is shadowed by darkness; therefore, I know that this is a spiritual battle. I will not fear, for You are faithful, and You will strengthen and protect me from the evil one! Thank you, Father, for protecting and shielding me from photos and information of the perpetrator.

AMEN

Your Turn

My Gratitude List
Recount God's blessings today

Date: _____

| Morning | Afternoon | Evening |

My Prayer List
Surrender your concerns to God

Date: _____

| Morning | Afternoon | Evening |

Deliverance From & Against Nightmares

You will not be afraid when you go to bed, and you will sleep soundly through the night. For the Spirit God gave us does not make us timid, but gives us power, love and self-discipline.
PROVERBS 3:24 GNT & 2 TIMOTHY 1:7 NIV

Jesus, I declare Your word over my life right now as I am struggling to sleep because of the traumas that I have endured. I pray that when I lie down, I will not be afraid; when I lie down, my sleep shall be sweet! I declare this right now, over my mind, over my sleep, and over my life! Lord, thank you. You have not given me this spirit of fear, but of power, and a sound mind. Thank you, Father, for delivering me from and against nightmares and for the ability to sleep and rest.

AMEN

Your Turn

My Gratitude List
Recount God's blessings today

Date: _____

Morning | Afternoon | Evening

My Prayer List
Surrender your concerns to God

Date: _____

Morning | Afternoon | Evening

Financial Provision For Medical Costs

My God will richly fill your every need in a glorious way through Christ Jesus. He is our refuge and strength, always ready to help in times of trouble.
PHILIPPIANS 4:19 GWT & PSALM 46:1 NLT

Jehovah Jireh, my Provider, I thank You in advance for meeting all my needs according to Your glorious riches. I know that although I may go through a financial strain to cover my medical costs and treatments, I know that I should continue to put my trust in You because You will always be faithful. I pray for more financial resources and divine strength from You to make it through; I put my trust in You as my Provider. Please continue to be my refuge and strength, an ever-present help in trouble.

AMEN

Your Turn

My Gratitude List
Recount God's blessings today

Date: _____

Morning | Afternoon | Evening

My Prayer List
Surrender your concerns to God

Date: _____

Morning | Afternoon | Evening

Guidance During The Legal Process

...no weapon forged against you will prevail, and you will refute every tongue that accuses you. This is the heritage of the servants of the LORD, and this is their vindication from me. declares the LORD.

ISAIAH 54:17 NIV

Omniscient Father, I ask for Your help and guidance during the legal processes of my journey. I know that You will surround me with great people who know what they are doing legally and I ask that the Holy Spirit give them the right words to say when they need them. Lord deliver me from lying tongue, deceitful lips, and hate. Help me Lord to hold my peace and allow you to fight this battle for me. Lord, let truth prevail. I believe and declare that no weapon formed against me will prosper, for surely You, O LORD, bless the righteous; You surround them with the shield of Your favor. Thank You for fighting this battle for me and for being a very present help in the time of trouble.

AMEN

Your Turn

My Gratitude List
Recount God's blessings today

Date: _____

| Morning | Afternoon | Evening |

My Prayer List
Surrender your concerns to God

Date: _____

| Morning | Afternoon | Evening |

SUPPORTIVE AND RELIABLE RESOURCES

*The Lord is my best friend and my shepherd.
I always have more than enough.*

PSALM 23:1 TPT

Awesome God, I pray that You bless me with a reliable support system for this long journey that I am about to endure. Father, I will continue to seek You in faith, because Your word says that those who seek You lack no good thing! Father, I ask You because I know that You will sustain me with a reliable support system for the long haul. I thank You in advance for seeing my needs and blessing me accordingly.

AMEN

My Gratitude List
Recount God's blessings today

Date: _____

Morning | Afternoon | Evening

My Prayer List
Surrender your concerns to God

Date: _____

Morning | Afternoon | Evening

Backing From Another Survivor

Iron sharpens iron, so one man sharpens another.
PROVERBS 27:17 NASB

God of Peace, I pray for the excellent support from another survivor, let it be healthy, and filled with love, understanding and patience. I pray that the words of my mouth and the thoughts of my heart will be pleasing to You, O Lord, my rock, and my redeemer. As iron sharpens iron, I pray that we both choose our words carefully so that we may only edify each other and not tear one another down. The well-known phrase is that "hurt people *hurt* people," but I declare instead that we healed people shall heal people.

AMEN

My Gratitude List
Recount God's blessings today

Date: _____

Morning | Afternoon | Evening

My Prayer List
Surrender your concerns to God

Date: _____

Morning | Afternoon | Evening

PROTECTION AGAINST RE-TRAUMATIZATION

He shall cover you with His feathers,
And under His wings you shall take refuge;
His truth *shall be your* shield and [a]buckler.
You shall not be afraid of the terror by night,
Nor of the arrow *that* flies by day,
Nor of the pestilence *that* walks in darkness,
Nor of the destruction *that* lays waste at noonday.

PSALM 91:4-6 NKJV

Righteous God, I pray against re-traumatization regardless of any future injuries. I declare that I will be covered by Your pinions, and under Your wings, I will find refuge. Your faithfulness is my shield and buckler! I will not fear the terror of the night, nor the arrow that flies by day, nor the destruction that wastes at noonday! You are my God, my Protector, and my Healer, I declare this so that any seed of re-traumatization may be destroyed.

AMEN

Your Turn

My Gratitude List
Recount God's blessings today

Date: _____

Morning	Afternoon	Evening

My Prayer List
Surrender your concerns to God

Date: _____

Morning	Afternoon	Evening

OPEN HEART TO CONNECT TO GOD

I long to drink of you, O God,
drinking deeply from the streams of pleasure
flowing from your presence. My longings overwhelm me for more of you! My soul thirsts, pants, and longs for the living God. I want to come and see the face of God.

PSALMS 42:1-5

Eternal Father, I pray that I open my heart to You like the Psalmist David did. Just as the deer pants for the streams of water, let my soul thirst for You. Yes, my tears have been my food day and night, while people ask me, "Where is your God?" but I pray that I continue to open my heart to You. I pray that I will not let my soul be downcast by the trials and traumas of the world. I will put my hope in You and praise You because You are my Savior and my God.

AMEN

My Gratitude List

Date: _____

Recount God's blessings today

| Morning | Afternoon | Evening |

My Prayer List

Date: _____

Surrender your concerns to God

| Morning | Afternoon | Evening |

Wisdom In My Decision Making

And the Spirit of the LORD shall rest upon him, the Spirit of wisdom and understanding, the Spirit of counsel and might, the Spirit of knowledge and the fear of the LORD.
ISAIAH 11:2 ESV

Heavenly Father, I pray that I become even more sensitive to Your Spirit so that I may discern what to do next with divine wisdom. I pray that I do not forsake wisdom, for she will protect me; I will love wisdom so that she will watch over me. Help me get knowledge and understanding, though it may cost all that I have because wisdom will help me do the correct thing in such a sensitive period in my life. It is easy to act upon emotions, but Lord, I want to walk in wisdom. For You say in your word that the first step to becoming wise is to look for wisdom, so use everything you have to get understanding. *Proverbs 4:6-7 ERV*

AMEN

My Gratitude List
Recount God's blessings today

Date: _____

Morning | Afternoon | Evening

My Prayer List
Surrender your concerns to God

Date: _____

Morning | Afternoon | Evening

Open Eyes To See God's Direction

Then Elisha prayed and said, "Lord, I ask you, open my servant's eyes so that he can see." The Lord opened the eyes of the young man, and the servant saw the mountain was full of horses and chariots of fire. They were all around Elisha.

2 KINGS 6:17 ERV

Marvelous God, I pray that You open my eyes so that I may see You in all of Your glory in my life. Elisha prayed and said, "O Lord, please open his eyes that he may see." And You opened the eyes of the young man who then saw the mountain full of horses and chariots of fire all around Elisha. Father, please open my eyes so that I can see the spiritual footprint manifest here on earth. Let me not focus on what I can see, but help me fix my focus on the unseen.

AMEN

Your Turn

My Gratitude List
Recount God's blessings today

Date: _____

Morning | Afternoon | Evening

My Prayer List
Surrender your concerns to God

Date: _____

Morning | Afternoon | Evening

Strength To Love Again

*Love is a safe place of shelter,
for it never stops believing the best for others.
Love never takes failure as defeat, for it never gives up.*

1 CORINTHIANS 13:7 TPT

God of Love, Your word says that I can have many things, but without love, the things that I have are nothing, and I am complete in You. Love is a fundamental part of being who You have called me to be, so please give me the strength to love again. I have been hurt repeatedly and severely by those around me, but please help me to love in my actions and in truth, not just with words or speech.

AMEN

Your Turn

My Gratitude List
Recount God's blessings today

Date: _____

| Morning | Afternoon | Evening |

My Prayer List
Surrender your concerns to God

Date: _____

| Morning | Afternoon | Evening |

Success In My Healing Journey

Lord, how wonderfully you bless the righteous.
Your favor wraps around each one and covers them
under your canopy of kindness and joy.

PSALMS 5:12 TPT

Precious God, I thank You in advance for Your favor upon me and the success that I will walk into as I travel the healing path! Surely You bless the righteous, and You surround them with Your favor as a shield! I pray that I continue to walk in Your shield of favor. I also pray that I will not let my trauma disqualify me from my success, because Your word states that if I commit to You whatever I do, my plans will succeed.

AMEN

Your Turn

My Gratitude List
Recount God's blessings today

Date: _____

Morning	Afternoon	Evening

My Prayer List
Surrender your concerns to God

Date: _____

Morning	Afternoon	Evening

REPRIEVE FROM NEGATIVE TRIGGERS

God, I invite your searching gaze into my heart. Examine me through and through; find out everything that may be hidden within me. Put me to the test and sift through all my anxious cares. See if there is any path of pain I'm walking on, and lead me back to your glorious, everlasting ways— the path that brings me back to you.

PSALMS 139:23

Awesome Father, I pray for deliverance from ongoing negative triggers. Even after going through my trauma, the pain still lingers and I pray for deliverance from this pain and from the triggers that surround me. I pray that I will keep my thoughts continually fixed on all that is authentic and real, honorable and admirable, beautiful and respectful, pure and holy, merciful and kind. I also pray that I will fasten my thoughts on every glorious work of God, praising You always. Lord, sift through all my anxious cares. See if there is any path of pain I'm walking on, that's causing these triggers and lead me back to your glorious, everlasting ways— the path that brings me back to you.

AMEN

My Gratitude List

Date: _____

Recount God's blessings today

Morning | Afternoon | Evening

My Prayer List

Date: _____

Surrender your concerns to God

Morning | Afternoon | Evening

WILLINGNESS TO EMBRACE GOD'S WILL

You formed my innermost being, shaping my delicate inside and my intricate outside, and wove them all together in my mother's womb. I thank you, God, for making me so mysteriously complex! Everything you do is marvelously breathtaking. It simply amazes me to think about it! How thoroughly you know me, Lord!
PSALMS 139:13

God of Creation, I pray that I see things like You do! Your word says that I am fearfully and wonderfully made, so please help me to see myself this way. The traumas and tribulations that I have encountered have caused me to believe in the opposite of who You have declared me to be. But Lord, I pray that You help me to embrace who You say I am, help me to understand that every good thing comes from above; comes from You, the Father of Lights.
AMEN

Your Turn

My Gratitude List
Recount God's blessings today

Date: _____

Morning | Afternoon | Evening

My Prayer List
Surrender your concerns to God

Date: _____

Morning | Afternoon | Evening

Patience With My Supporters

Love is large and incredibly patient. Love is gentle and consistently kind to all. It refuses to be jealous when blessing comes to someone else. Love does not brag about one's achievements nor inflate its own importance.

1 CORINTHIANS 13:4 TPT

Author of my life, I pray that You fill my heart with love today because Your word tells me that love is patient and kind. I pray for an increase of Your love so that I may exercise patience with those who do not understand PTSD. You know me better than anybody else, you understand the groaning that I have that cannot be expressed in words. On the other hand, people do not know me to this deep level and may not understand, so help me to exercise patience. Holy Spirit, please take hold of us in our human frailty and empower us in our weakness. For example, at times when we don't even know how to pray, or know the best things to ask for. Holy Spirit rise up within us and super-intercede on our behalf, in Jesus's name.

AMEN

My Gratitude List
Recount God's blessings today

Date: _____

Morning	Afternoon	Evening

My Prayer List
Surrender your concerns to God

Date: _____

Morning	Afternoon	Evening

Hedge Of Protection Over My Children

But the Lord Yahweh is always faithful to place you on
a firm foundation and guard you from the Evil One.
2 THESSALONIANS 3:3 TPT

Mighty Warrior, there is nothing in this world that can thwart your mighty power. I pray against the evil forces that is around me that I cannot battle by myself right now. Lord, I bow down to You and Your authority, asking that You protect me from this curse and prevent it from reaching third or fourth generations in my bloodline. I pray against this curse and declare that the blood breaks it off the lamb in Jesus' name. It shall no longer manifest in my family or me, in Jesus' Name. Your word says that no weapon fashioned against me shall succeed, and I will refute every tongue that rises against me in judgment. As I walk amid evil, Lord, please preserve my life; stretch out your hand against the wrath of my enemies, and deliver me with your right hand, in Jesus' name.

AMEN

My Gratitude List

Date: _____

Recount God's blessings today

Morning	Afternoon	Evening

My Prayer List

Date: _____

Surrender your concerns to God

Morning	Afternoon	Evening

PRAYERS FROM THE THREAD BOOK

Ability To Think Good Thoughts

Likewise, the Spirit helps us in our weakness. For we do not know what to pray for as we ought, but the Spirit himself intercedes for us with groaning too deep for words.
ROMANS 8:26 ESV

Creator of the universe, I am calling on the personal power, support, and resources given to me by You, my God, in the form of the Holy Spirit. I am ready to allow You in. I thank You for opening my eyes to see that I can overcome my past and be made whole. Please help me to break free from those chains of bondage created by the past traumatic experiences that are holding me back from fulfilling my purpose in You. Please also forgive me for everything I've done that was not pleasing in Your sight. Thank You for freeing me from fear so that I can boldly break my silence, face the truth about what has happened to me, and start anew. Thank You for freeing me from the condemnation and shame of abuse and allowing me to walk forward in the newness of Christ. I Thank You that old things have passed away and that I am a new creature in You. No longer will I be a victim of shame, guilt, humiliation, or fear, but I am victorious through the power of my testimony. Thank You, Lord, for victory, freedom, and new beginnings. I declare that I am a courageous woman. In Jesus' name.
AMEN

Your Turn

My Gratitude List

Recount God's blessings today

Date: _____

Morning	Afternoon	Evening

My Prayer List

Surrender your concerns to God

Date: _____

Morning	Afternoon	Evening

WILLINGNESS TO LEARN FROM THE PAST

When the Spirit of truth comes, he will guide you into all the truth, for he will not speak on his own authority, but whatever he hears he will speak, and he will declare to you the things that are to come.

JOHN 16:13 ESV

Papa, thank You for bestowing the Holy Spirit within me so that I can be powerful from within according to Your example. Lord, thank You for being the God of second chances. Thank You for being a God who does not condemn, but who is always willing to show us grace, mercy, compassion, and forgiveness. Lord, please take everything out of me that is not pleasing to you and help me to see what steps I need to take to prevent myself from making the kind of poor decisions I've made in my past. Please help me to overcome the lasting effects of my trauma that have caused me to feel useless, hopeless, or worthless. Lord, I believe that there is no situation too painful, shameful, or difficult for You to change. I pray that You would create in me a clean heart and renew a right spirit within me. Please forgive me for the mistakes I made as a result of not knowing and recognizing the truth. You are the way, the truth, and the life. Thank You for healing my heart and granting me Your peace today. I declare that my mind is renewed in Jesus' name.

AMEN

Your Turn

My Gratitude List

Date: _____

Recount God's blessings today

Morning | Afternoon | Evening

My Prayer List

Date: _____

Surrender your concerns to God

Morning | Afternoon | Evening

HELP TO RELEASE THE TRAUMA

Let all bitterness and wrath and anger and clamour and slander be put away from you, along with all malice. Be kind to one another, tender-hearted, forgiving one another, as God in Christ forgave you.

EPHESIANS 4:31

Architect of my future, I thank You for Your words of comfort and healing that have brought life to my situation today. Thank You for reminding me that I am loved, valued, accepted, and beautiful. Thank You for giving me access to a love that will never leave me thirsty, a love that I didn't have to do anything to be worthy of. God, I pray that You help me to see myself the way that You see me. Please help me to overcome the debilitating effects of my past that caused me to feel unworthy, unloved, and unwanted. I know that I am worthy because You deem me fit. I am loved and adored by You. I surrender everything I have—my mind, heart, body, soul, and spirit—to You. No longer will I live in regret for the things I endured that were no fault of my own. I now recognize that I am worthy of greater love and for I was given than I have received or accepted from others. Please create in me a clean heart and renew a right spirit in me so that I can rise to the purpose You have created for my life. I thank You that you fearfully and wonderfully made me, and I will walk in the confidence and truth that I am a child of the Most High God. This is a new beginning for me, and I will walk in newness. No longer will I be a victim of my past defeats because I declare that I am victorious. In Jesus' name,
AMEN

Your Turn

My Gratitude List

Recount God's blessings today

Date: _____

Morning	Afternoon	Evening

My Prayer List

Surrender your concerns to God

Date: _____

Morning	Afternoon	Evening

DIRECTION TO CHOOSE THE RIGHT ALLIES

Where there is no [wise, intelligent] guidance, the people fall [and go off course like a ship without a helm], but in the abundance of [wise and godly] counselors there is victory.

PROVERBS 11:14 AMP

Sovereign God, I thank You so much for allowing me to see the potential and the purpose that You have placed inside of me in the form of Your Holy Spirit. I thank You for opening my eyes to know that I do not have to walk this path alone. I pray that You would bless me with the right allies and mentors to help me continue to grow on my journey to a rewarding experience. I relinquish the pain, guilt, and shame of my past and choose to focus on my future in You. I stand and proclaim that I am worthy of love, joy, and peace, and I thank You for supplying every one of my needs. You are wonderful and worthy of all glory, honour, and praise. Thank You for blessing me with true friends whom I can trust to assist me in being accountable to the new positive changes that I have made. I declare new beginnings. In Jesus' name.

AMEN

Your Turn

My Gratitude List
Recount God's blessings today

Date: _____

| Morning | Afternoon | Evening |

My Prayer List
Surrender your concerns to God

Date: _____

| Morning | Afternoon | Evening |

READINESS TO ADOPT NEW MINDSET AND BEHAVIORS

Let my passion for life be restored, tasting joy in every breakthrough you bring to me. Hold me close to you with a willing spirit that obeys whatever you say.
PSALMS 51:12 TPT

Living God, Thank You so much for showing me that healing and recovery are possible. Thank You for protecting and preserving my life and for not allowing my trauma to ruin me. Lord, please help me to find my hope, joy, and peace in You. Remind me always that I am filled with Your Holy Spirit, and don't allow my circumstances to take away my strength, happiness, or purpose. Please help me adopt a new mindsets and behaviours that will assist me in my recovery, physically, mentally, spiritually, and emotionally. Help me activate my faith in the healing power of Jesus Christ, knowing that He has the power to make me whole again. I thank You that there is nothing too hard for You and that by believing in Your power and utilizing resources to help me overcome my traumatic experiences every day, I declare I am stronger and wiser. In Jesus' name.
AMEN

Your Turn

My Gratitude List

Date: _____

Recount God's blessings today

Morning | Afternoon | Evening

My Prayer List

Date: _____

Surrender your concerns to God

Morning | Afternoon | Evening

Desire To Dream Again

Remember not the former things, nor consider the things of old. Behold, I am doing a new thing; now it springs forth, do you not perceive it? I will make a way in the wilderness and rivers in the desert.

ISAIAH 43:18

My sweet Jesus, I am so grateful for how these words are truly awakening a fire inside of me and showing me that I can and will make a better life for myself out of these scraps that You have shown me are not useless. I pray that You take the scraps of my life and transform them into useable works of art that will help others see how awesome and mighty You are. I am Your willing vessel. Lord, thank You for inspiring me to dream differently and to know that You are eager to bless me with more than I could even imagine. Thank You for Your Word. Please remove every remaining shred of guilt and shame that tries to keep me from fully embracing my dreams. Show me the dreams that You have placed in my heart and guide me in fulfilling them. I thank You that my dreams are bigger than I am—that they will last forever, meet someone else's need, and bring glory to Your name. Please help me to do everything unto You and not for my selfish gain. Thank You for instilling in me the desire to expand my horizons as You enlarge my territory. I declare my freedom to live true happiness in Christ. I give You all the glory, honour, and praise. In Jesus' name.

AMEN

Your Turn

My Gratitude List
Recount God's blessings today

Date: _____

Morning | Afternoon | Evening

My Prayer List
Surrender your concerns to God

Date: _____

Morning | Afternoon | Evening

Commitment To Discover My Gifts

I keep running hard toward the finish line to get the prize that is mine because God has called me through Christ Jesus to life up there in heaven.
PHILIPPIANS 3:14 ERV

Reliable God, thank You so much for how You have awakened a fire inside of me that makes me want to thrive in my purpose. Please show me any hidden, undiscovered, or ignored gifts that You have placed inside of me so I can draw them out and begin working them. Help me to not compare myself to others or feel that any of my gifts are small or insignificant. I know that every gift and every person have a purpose, so please help me keep my eyes on You and stay in my lane. Thank You for the gifts that You have entrusted in me. Please help me use them to glorify You and not for any selfish or ulterior motive. Give me the grace to work multiple gifts without becoming burned out or overwhelmed. Thank You for Your hand on my life and for choosing me for Your unique and magnificent purpose. I thank You that I am fearfully and wonderfully made. I thank You that I am a daughter of the King of Kings. Thank You for the great and mighty things that are getting ready to come. In Jesus' name.
AMEN

Your Turn

My Gratitude List
Recount God's blessings today

Date: _____

| Morning | Afternoon | Evening |

My Prayer List
Surrender your concerns to God

Date: _____

| Morning | Afternoon | Evening |

Desire To Live A Joyful Life In Christ

Then he said to them, "Go your way. Eat the fat and drink sweet wine and send portions to anyone who has nothing ready, for this day is holy to our Lord. And do not be grieved, for the joy of the Lord is your strength."
NEHEMIAH 8:10 ESV

Everlasting Father, Thank You so much for showing me that nothing I have experienced has been in vain and that I do not have to be bound to the shame of my past. Thank You for Your healing and redeeming power to not only set me free but to use me to help set others free. I thank You that Your plan and purpose for my life is good and that my destiny is already prepared for me. Even when I don't understand everything, I choose to allow You to use me for Your glory, knowing that when my life is in Your hands, You work everything together for my good. I am not a victim; I am a victor. I am beautiful, successful, and loved by You. I look forward to the next step and the next phase of my life. I will embrace this journey with an open mind and heart. I will be positive and hopeful, knowing that I am worthy of blessings and prosperity. Thank You for how You have opened my eyes to the truth about myself and whom You made me to be. In Jesus' name.
AMEN

Your Turn

My Gratitude List
Recount God's blessings today

Date: _____

| Morning | Afternoon | Evening |

My Prayer List
Surrender your concerns to God

Date: _____

| Morning | Afternoon | Evening |

Courage To Walk In My Purpose

But you are his chosen people, the King's priests. You are a holy nation, people who belong to God. He chose you to tell about the wonderful things he has done. He brought you out of the darkness of sin into his wonderful light.

1 PETER 2:9 ERV

King of my life, I need You to renew a right spirit within me. I want to have a right spirit. I want to be safe to love. I'm tired of hurting others and I'm tired of the hurt I'm carrying myself. I want to be a better woman. Have mercy on me, my Lord, and make me a better woman. I want to be made whole. Please, Lord, make me over again. I surrender everything to You—my heart, mind, body, spirit, soul, and all my useless scraps. I know there is nothing too hard for You. I'm ready to break up with my past once and for all and start over from this day forward. I will no longer be defined by my past and I want You to craft my destiny. I want to walk in purpose and help others overcome their troubles through the power of my testimony. I am an overcomer. I am beautiful. I am loved and treasured by the King. I am part of a royal priesthood. Today is my new beginning. Today is my fresh start. Today I can and will be made whole. I thank You, Lord, for showing me who You are. Through knowing the truth of who You are and what You've done for me, I see myself clearly. I see that You've been with me all along, protecting, covering, and keeping me. Thank You for providing for me. Thank You for being a Healer and a Waymaker. Thank You for this brand-new day. Thank You for creating a beautiful masterpiece out of all my life experiences. In Jesus' name.

AMEN

Your Turn

My Gratitude List
Recount God's blessings today

Date: _____

| Morning | Afternoon | Evening |

My Prayer List
Surrender your concerns to God

Date: _____

| Morning | Afternoon | Evening |

Freedom To Live True Happiness

It is for freedom that Christ has set us free. Stand firm, then, and do not let yourselves be burdened again by a yoke of slavery.

GALATIANS 5:1

Faithful Father, there are areas in my life where I've been held captive, and I may still be captive to some things. I'm here because I need You to set me free from all of them. I need Your loving compassion to restore my soul as I walk in the freedom You have provided for me through Christ. In Jesus' name I pray.

AMEN

Your Turn

My Gratitude List

Date: _____

Recount God's blessings today

Morning | Afternoon | Evening

My Prayer List

Date: _____

Surrender your concerns to God

Morning | Afternoon | Evening

EPHESIANS 1:18-20 TPT

How are you feeling? I trust that you will continue to delight yourself in the Lord and use Bible scriptures as part of your everyday living and loving yourself and others to God.

Are you saved? If not, I'm inviting you to come to Christ and take Him as your personal Saviour. Please know, being saved will not remove all your problems, but it does give you a Saviour Who will carry you through them! Would you pray and ask Jesus to be your Saviour? If so, please pray something like this:

"**Dear Jesus, I know I am a sinner, and that means I am separated from You, and I deserve Hell. I am sorry for my sin. By Your grace, I want to turn from my sin- all of it- and give You my life. I believe that You died for my sins, and that faith in You is the only way to be saved. I confess that You are the risen Lord and Saviour, and I ask You to come into my heart and save me from my sins. Thank You for saving me. Thank You for loving me. Please give me the strength to live my new life for You. I pray this in Your name. AMEN.**

If you have just received Christ as your Saviour, you have made the most important step in your life! You can now have confidence that you build a personal relationship with Jesus and He will help you to overcome, the sins of this life. Most importantly, living for Christ is a sure way of you spending eternity in Heaven with Jesus.

As a next step, it is important that you remember this time when you received Christ. Write today's date as the day of your salvation. Do you need a bible? If so, please contact me at leonie@leoniemattison.com

Above all, "I pray that the light of God will illuminate the eyes of your imagination, flooding you with light, until you experience the full revelation of the hope of his calling—that is, the wealth of God's glorious inheritances that he finds in us, his holy ones! I decree that you will continually experience the immeasurable greatness of God's power made available to you through faith. I declare that your lives will be an advertisement of this immense power as it works through you! May the mighty power that was released when God raised Christ from the dead, exalt you to the place of highest honor and supreme authority in the heavenly realm!"

EPHESIANS 1:18-20 TPT

LOOKING FOR MORE RESOURCES

- Visit: www.leoniemattison.com as often as you wish
- Download a free audio version of the first five prayers from this book
- Purchase the audio version of this book on my website at www.leoniemattison.com/store/
- Check out The Thread Collection
    - The Thread: Let God into Your Life & Achieve Intentional Transformation
    - The Thread Adult Colouring Book with Bible Scriptures
    - The Thread Adult Colouring Book with Uplifting Quotes
    - Beside Still Waters: 21 Day Devotional
- Coming Soon
    - 30 Prayers for Trauma Survivors
    - Wait in Him: 31 Day Devotion

About The Author

Dr. Leonie H Mattison is a devout Christian, trauma survivor, and author of *The Thread* collection: self-help book, 21-day devotional, adult coloring book, six-step healing tool, 30-day prayer book, and children's illustrated book.

She has a passion for Christ and wants to see survivors heal so they can live the life Christ intended. She and her children are devoted to the local church and have the privilege of serving her community as a teacher, mentor, and speaker.

Leonie believes her calling is to help dispirited women win back their power by connecting them to the redemptive love and transforming power of Christ. She is a busy single mom and business executive, but one commitment remains constant, she says. *"I can do all things through Christ who strengthens me."* Philippians 4:28

CONNECT WITH DR. LEONIE H. MATTISON
Facebook@Leoniehmattison
Instagram@Leoniehmattison
Twitter:Leoniemattison
Website: www.leoniemattison.com

Made in the USA
Middletown, DE
12 May 2024